CONTENTS

THE JUNGLE BOOK

Retold from

Rudyard Kipling

by Jane B. Mason and Sarah Hines Stephens

SCHOLASTIC INC.

ISBN 978-0-439-57424-2

Based on *The Jungle Book* by Rudyard Kipling, which was first published in 1894.

5 4 3 2 1   18 19 20 21

Printed in the U.S.A.   40

Mowgli's Brothers

IT was seven o'clock on a warm evening. Father Wolf woke from his day's rest, yawned, and stretched his paws to get rid of the sleepy feeling in their tips. Mother Wolf lay with her big gray nose across her four tumbling, squealing cubs. The moon shone into the mouth of the cave where they all lived.

"Aurgh!" said Father Wolf. "It's time to hunt again." He was about to spring down the hill when a little shadow with a bushy tail stepped into the cave.

"Good luck go with you, Chief of the Wolves. May your noble children have strong white teeth. And may they never forget those who are hungry," the shadow whined. It was the dish licker, Tabaqui the Jackal.

The wolves of India despised Tabaqui because he ran around making mischief, telling tales, and eating rags from the village rubbish heaps. But they were afraid of him, too. Of all the animals in the jungle, Tabaqui was the most likely to go mad. And when he was mad he forgot to be afraid of anyone and ran around biting everything in his way. Even the tiger ran and hid when little Tabaqui went mad.

"Come in and have a look," Father Wolf said stiffly, "but there is no food here."

"Maybe not for a wolf, but for me a dry bone is a feast. Who are the Jackal People to pick and choose?" Tabaqui scuttled to the back of the cave. There he found a bone with a little meat on it and sat cracking the end merrily.

"Thanks for this good meal," Tabaqui said, licking his lips. His eyes turned to Mother Wolf and the four cubs. "What beautiful, noble children! What large eyes! And so young!"

Now, Tabaqui knew it was unlucky to compliment children to their faces, and it pleased him to see Mother and Father Wolf look uncomfortable. Tabaqui sat a moment, rejoicing in the mischief that he'd made. Then he went on, "Shere Kahn has shifted his hunting grounds. He told me he will hunt among these hills for the next moon."

Shere Kahn the Tiger lived near the Waingunga River, twenty miles away.

"He has no right!" Father Wolf said angrily. "By the Law of the Jungle he has no right to change his hunting grounds without warning. He will frighten all of the game for ten miles around."

"His mother did not call him Lungri, the Lame One, for nothing," said Mother Wolf quietly. "He has been lame in one foot since he was born. That is why he only kills cattle. The villagers of Waingunga have grown angry with him and now he has come here to make *our* villagers angry."

"Go and hunt with your master," Father Wolf told Tabaqui. "You've done enough harm here for one night."

As Tabaqui slunk out of the cave, Father Wolf heard the angry, snarly, singsong whine of a hungry tiger in the valley below.

"The fool!" Father Wolf snapped. "Beginning a night's hunting with that noise! Does he think our bucks are as easy to catch as his fat Waingunga bulls?"

"Hush! He is not hunting for bull or buck," said Mother Wolf. "Tonight he is hunting man."

The whine changed to a humming purr that seemed to come from all directions. It was the noise that bewilders woodcutters and sleeping Gypsies, making them walk into the very mouth of the tiger.

"Man!" said Father Wolf, showing his

teeth. "Aren't there enough beetles and frogs to feed him? He must eat man, and on our land?"

The Law of the Jungle states that no beast shall eat man. This is because when a beast eats a man, the rest of the man's village rides into the jungle with guns, gongs, rockets, and torches. Then everybody in the jungle suffers.

Shere Kahn's purr grew louder, ending in the full-throated growl of the tiger's charge. A moment later there was a pitiful howl.

"He missed," Mother Wolf said.

Father Wolf ran out of the cave and heard Shere Kahn muttering and mumbling savagely as he tumbled about in the bushes.

"The fool has jumped into a woodcutter's campfire and burned his feet," Father Wolf said with a grunt. "Tabaqui is with him."

"Something is coming up the hill,"

Mother Wolf said. Her ear twitched. "Get ready."

There was a rustling in the thicket. Father Wolf dropped to his haunches, ready to leap. He sprang forward, but when he saw what he was leaping at he tried to stop mid-jump. He shot up into the air four or five feet and landed almost exactly where he had left the ground.

"Man," he snapped. "A man-cub. Look!"

There in the thicket stood a naked brown baby who could only just walk. The soft, dimpled boy looked up into Father Wolf's face and laughed.

"Is that a man-cub?" asked Mother Wolf. "I have never seen one. Bring it here."

A wolf accustomed to carrying his own cubs can hold an egg in his mouth without breaking it. And though Father Wolf's jaws closed on the small child's back, not a tooth scratched the baby's skin as he laid the man-cub down among his own cubs.

"How little! How naked, and — how bold!" Mother Wolf said softly. The baby pushed his way between the wolf cubs to get close to Mother's warm fur. "The man-cub is taking his milk with the others!" she said with surprise. "Now, was there ever a wolf who could boast of a man-cub among her children?"

"I have heard of it now and again. But never in our pack, or in my time," Father Wolf replied. "He is completely without hair and I could kill him with a touch of my paw. But see, he looks up and is not afraid."

Suddenly, the cave grew darker. The moonlight was blocked by the tiger Shere Kahn. His great square head and shoulders filled the cave's entrance. Tabaqui was behind him squeaking, "My lord, my lord, it went in here!"

"You honor us with your presence, Shere Kahn," Father Wolf said, but his eyes were angry. "What do you need?"

"A man-cub went this way," said Shere Kahn, growling from the pain in his burned feet. "Its parents have run off. Give it to me."

Shere Kahn looked threatening, but Father Wolf knew that the mouth of the cave was too narrow for a tiger to fit through.

"I will not take orders from you, Shere Kahn," said Father Wolf. "A wolf takes orders from the pack leader, and not from any striped cattle killer. The man-cub is ours to kill if we choose."

"What is this talk of choosing? How dare you deny me what is rightfully mine? It is I, Shere Kahn, who speaks!" The tiger's roar filled the cave like booming thunder.

Mother Wolf shook herself free of the cubs and sprang forward. Her eyes resembled two green moons in the darkness. "And it is I, Raksha, the Demon, who answers. The man-cub is mine, Lungri! He shall not be killed. He shall live to run and

10

hunt with the pack. Look well, hunter of naked cubs, for one day he will hunt *you*! Now go back to where you came from, lamer than you were when you came into the world. Go!"

Father Wolf looked on, amazed. He had almost forgotten the day he had won Mother Wolf in a fight against five other wolves. Back then she had run in the pack, and she was not called the Demon by accident. Shere Kahn might have faced Father Wolf, but he could not stand up against Raksha. She had all of the advantage of ground and would fight to the death. So, Shere Kahn backed out of the cave.

When he was clear, the tiger shouted, "We will see what the pack has to say about raising man-cubs. He will come to my teeth in the end, you bush-tailed thieves!"

Mother Wolf lay down among the cubs, panting.

"Some of what Shere Kahn says is true," Father Wolf said. "We must show the cub to the pack. Do you still want to keep him?"

"He came naked, at night, alone and very hungry," Mother Wolf said, "but he was not afraid. Shere Kahn would have killed him then run off while the villagers hunted our cubs in revenge! Keep him? Of course I will keep him. Lie still, Little Frog. Mowgli the Frog, that's what I'll call you. The day will come when you will hunt Shere Kahn as he has hunted you."

"But what will our pack say?" Father Wolf asked.

The Law of the Jungle says that every wolf must bring his cubs before the pack council as soon as they are old enough to stand. They are brought so that the other wolves can identify them, and, once they have been inspected, the cubs are allowed to run free. No grown wolf is allowed to harm a cub until he has killed his first buck.

On the next full moon, Father Wolf, his

cubs, Mowgli, and Mother Wolf went to Council Rock. The strong and clever pack leader, Akela, lay full length on one of the hundred rocks covering the hill. Below him sat forty more wolves of every size and color.

There was very little talking at the Rock. Cubs tumbled over one another inside the circle made up of their mothers and fathers. Now and then a senior wolf would quietly go up to a cub, look at him carefully, and then return to his spot on noiseless feet. Sometimes a mother would push her cub into the moonlight to make sure he had not been overlooked.

From his rock Akela called out, "You know the Law. Look well, O wolves."

The anxious mothers took up the call. "Look. Look well, O wolves!"

At last Father Wolf pushed Mowgli into the center, where he laughed and played with some pebbles that glistened in the moonlight.

Akela did not raise his head from his paws but continued to cry, "Look well!"

A muffled roar came from behind the rocks. Shere Kahn! "The cub is mine," he called. "Give him to me! What does the wolf pack want with a man-cub?"

Akela did not even twitch his ears. He simply said, "Look well, O wolves. The pack does not take orders from anyone save ourselves. Look well."

There was a chorus of deep growls. A four-year-old wolf repeated Shere Kahn's question. "What does the pack want with a man-cub?"

According to the Law of the Jungle, a cub in question will be accepted into the pack if he is spoken for by at least two pack members who are not his mother or father.

"Who speaks for this cub?" Akela asked. There was no answer. Mother Wolf got ready for a fight — if it came to that.

Then the only other creature allowed at

the pack council — Baloo, the sleepy brown bear who teaches the cubs the Law of the Jungle — rose up on his hindquarters and grunted.

"The man-cub?" he said. "I'll speak for him. There is no harm in a man-cub. Let him run with the pack and be accepted with the others. I myself will teach him."

"We need one more," Akela said. "Baloo has spoken and he is our cubs' teacher. Who besides Baloo?"

A black shadow dropped down into the circle. It was inky-black Bagheera the Panther. Everybody knew Bagheera, and nobody dared cross him. Bagheera was as clever as Tabaqui, as bold as a water buffalo, and as reckless as a wounded elephant. But he had a voice as sweet as wild honey dripping from a tree and skin softer than down.

"Akela and the wolves," he purred, "I have no right at your council, but the Law of the Jungle says if there is a cub in question that cub may be bought for a price. And the Law does not say who may or may not pay that price, am I correct?"

"Mmm. Yes," said the young wolves, for they were always hungry and hoped Bagheera would offer food. "Speak."

"It would be a shame to kill a naked cub. Besides, he will make better sport when he is grown. To Baloo's word I add one water buffalo, a fat one, newly killed, not half a mile from here. Will you accept the man-cub according to the Law?"

Many wolves spoke at once. "What does it matter? He will die in the winter rains."

"He will burn in the sun."

"How can a naked frog hurt us?"

"Let him run with the pack."

"Where is the buffalo, Bagheera?"

And then came Akela's cry, "Look well. Look well, O wolves."

Mowgli was still engrossed in the pebbles. He did not even notice as the wolves looked him over one by one and then

16

padded softly down the hill toward the dead buffalo. Soon only Akela, Bagheera, Baloo, and Mowgli's own wolf family were left.

Shere Kahn roared angrily in the distance.

"Roar well," Bagheera said under his whiskers. "A time will come when this cub will make you roar another tune, Shere Kahn, or I know nothing of man."

"Well done," Akela said. "Men and their cubs are wise. He may be a help in time." Akela was thinking of the time that comes to every pack leader, when his strength leaves him and he gets feebler and feebler until at last he is killed and a new leader emerges. "Take him away," Akela said to Father Wolf. "Train him as one of us."

Over the next ten or eleven years, Mowgli had many wonderful adventures among the wolves. He grew up with the cubs, though they were grown wolves before he was even a child. Father Wolf and Baloo the Bear taught him all the things to know in the jungle. When Mowgli was not learning, he sat in the sun and slept and ate and slept again. When he felt hot or dirty, he swam in the forest pools. And when he wanted honey (Baloo taught him that honey and nuts were as good to eat as meat), he climbed up and got it.

Mowgli was very good at climbing anywhere, thanks to Bagheera. When Mowgli was still very small, Bagheera would lie out on a branch and call, "Come along, Little Brother." At first, Mowgli would cling to a vine and crawl slowly along, but soon he could fling himself through the branches of the jungle as boldly as an ape.

When the pack met, Mowgli took his place at Council Rock. He discovered that if he stared hard at any wolf, the wolf would be forced to drop his eyes. In this way Mowgli could easily win any argument. But sometimes he would stare just for fun. He would also pick long, painful thorns out of the paws of his wolf friends. The members of the pack were grateful for Mowgli's nimble fingers, and Mowgli considered himself to be one of them.

At night, Mowgli would go down the hillside into the farmlands and look at the villagers in their huts. He was curious about men, but he did not trust them. Bagheera had shown him a trap made by men, so well hidden in the jungle that Mowgli had nearly walked into it.

There was nothing Mowgli liked better than to spend the day with Bagheera in the warm, dark heart of the forest. They would sleep all the drowsy day, and at night Mowgli would watch Bagheera do his hunting. Bagheera hunted easily whenever he felt hungry. And so did Mowgli — with one exception. As soon as Mowgli was old enough to understand, Bagheera had told him he must never harm water buffalo because he had been accepted into the pack for the price of a buffalo's life. "All the jungle is yours," Bagheera said. "But, for the sake of that bull, you must never kill or eat water buffalo. That is the Law of the Jungle." Mowgli obeyed the rule faithfully.

Mowgli grew big and strong, living the carefree life of a boy who thought mostly of things to eat.

Once or twice, Mother Wolf told him that Shere Kahn was not to be trusted. She told him that someday he must kill Shere Kahn. A young wolf would have remembered that advice every hour. But because he was only a boy, Mowgli forgot it.

Shere Kahn was always crossing Mowgli's path. The tiger had become great friends with the younger wolves in the pack, who followed him and ate his scraps. This was something Akela would never have allowed in his stronger days, but the pack leader was growing old and feeble.

Shere Kahn flattered the younger

wolves, asking them why such fine hunters were content to be led by a dying wolf and a man-cub. "They tell me at council you don't dare look him in the eyes," the tiger would say. And the young wolves would growl and bristle.

Bagheera, who had eyes and ears everywhere, tried to warn Mowgli that Shere Kahn was a dangerous enemy. But Mowgli just laughed. "I have you and the pack, and even lazy Baloo might strike a blow for my sake. Why should I be afraid?"

One very warm day, Bagheera tried again. "Little Brother, how often have I told you Shere Kahn is your enemy and will one day try to kill you?"

Mowgli lay with his head on Bagheera's beautiful black fur. "As many times as there are nuts on that palm," he replied. "But I am sleepy, and Shere Kahn is all long tail and loud talk, like Mao the Peacock."

"This is no time for sleeping," Bagheera said seriously. "Shere Kahn is a danger to you. Baloo knows and I know. The pack knows and even Tabaqui knows."

"Ho! Ho!" Mowgli laughed. "Tabaqui came to me with rude talk, and I swung him by the tail against a tree to teach him better manners."

"That was foolish," Bagheera said. "Tabaqui may be a mischief-maker, but he would have told you important things. Shere Kahn will not dare to kill you as long as Akela is the leader of the pack. But Akela is growing old. The day is coming when he will no longer lead. Many of the younger wolves believe, as Shere Kahn has taught them, that a man-cub has no place in the pack. And soon you will be a man."

"Why can't a man run with his brothers?" Mowgli asked. "I was born in the jungle. I obey the Law of the Jungle. I have pulled thorns from the paws of every wolf here. Surely they are my brothers!"

Bagheera stretched his full length. "Little Brother, feel under my chin," he said with half-closed eyes.

Mowgli put his hand under Bagheera's silky chin. Just under the jaw he found a little bald spot.

"There is no one in the jungle who knows that I, Bagheera, carry that mark. It is the mark of the collar. Yes, Little Brother, I have lived among men. It was among men that my mother died — in the cages of the king's palace. That is why I paid the price for you at the council when you were a naked cub. Like you, I was born among men. They fed me behind bars, until one day I knew I was Bagheera the Panther — and no man's plaything. With one blow from my paw, I broke the lock. I ran away, and, because I had learned the ways of men, I became more terrible in the jungle than even Shere Kahn. Isn't that so?"

"Yes," Mowgli nodded. "Everyone in the jungle fears Bagheera — except Mowgli."

"You *are* a man-cub," Bagheera said tenderly. "Just as I returned to the jungle, one day you will go back to the world of men . . . if you are not killed by the pack first."

"Why should the pack wish to kill me?" Mowgli asked.

"Look at me," said Bagheera. Mowgli looked steadily into his eyes. After half a minute, the big panther turned his head away. "*That* is why," Bagheera said. "Not even I can look you in the eyes, and I love you, Little Brother. The others hate you because their eyes cannot meet yours. They see that they are not your equal, because you are wise, because you have pulled thorns from their feet, because you are a man."

"I didn't know." Mowgli frowned under his heavy black brows.

"Be wise," Bagheera cautioned, "and be wary. When Akela misses his next kill, the pack will turn against him and against you. They will hold council at the Rock, and then . . . then . . . I have it!" Bagheera leaped up. "Go now, quickly, down to the men's huts and take some of the Red Flower they grow there. Then, when the time comes, you will have an even stronger friend than myself or Baloo or your brothers in the pack. Get the Red Flower."

Bagheera was talking about fire. No creature in the jungle called fire by its name, because every beast lived in fear of it.

"The Red Flower?" Mowgli repeated. "I have seen it growing outside men's huts at twilight. I will get some."

"Spoken like a man-cub!" Bagheera said

proudly. "Go swiftly. Get the Flower in a little pot and keep it beside you."

"I will go," Mowgli said, slipping an arm around his friend's neck and looking into his big eyes. "But tell me, Bagheera, are you sure this trouble is Shere Kahn's doing?"

"I swear on the broken lock that freed me, Little Brother," Bagheera answered.

"And I swear on the buffalo that bought me, I will repay him in full and maybe a little more." With that, Mowgli bounded away.

"That is man," Bagheera said to himself as he lay back down. "That is all man."

On his way down the hill, Mowgli stopped to listen to the pack hunting. He heard the bellow of a buck being chased. Then he heard the wicked, bitter howls of the young wolves. "Akela! Akela! Show your strength. Spring, Akela!" Mowgli heard the snap of Akela's teeth and then a yelp as the buck knocked him with his foot. The leader of the pack must have sprung and missed.

Mowgli did not wait to hear more. He dashed onward, the yells growing faint behind him. "Bagheera spoke the truth," he panted, hiding below the window of a hut. "Tomorrow fate will be decided for Akela — and for me. I must get the Red Flower to save us both!"

Mowgli watched through the window all night long as a woman tended the fire in the hearth, feeding it small black lumps to keep it burning. In the morning he saw a child pick up a pot. Being careful not to touch the charcoal with his hands, the child filled the small pot with the embers. Then he carried the pot with him as he stepped outside to tend the cattle.

"Is that all?" Mowgli said to himself. "If a cub can handle it, there is nothing to fear." He walked around the corner and took the pot from the boy's hand. Then, while the boy howled in fear, Mowgli disappeared into the mist.

Mowgli blew into the pot like he had seen the woman do. "This thing will die if I do not feed it," he said. He gave it twigs and dried bark to eat. The red coals sparked and flared.

Halfway up the hill, Mowgli met Bagheera. Morning dew shone like moonstones on the panther's coat.

"Akela missed," Bagheera said. "The pack would have killed him last night, but you were not there. They were looking for you on the hill. They will expect you at Council Rock tonight."

"I was down by the village. But I am ready." Mowgli held up the fire-pot.

"Good. I have seen men put a dry branch into the pot and make the Red Flower bloom on it. Aren't you afraid?" Bagheera said.

"Why should I be afraid?" Mowgli asked. "I remember, before I was a wolf, I used to lie beside the Red Flower. It was warm and pleasant."

All that day Mowgli sat in the cave tending his fire-pot, dipping dry branches into it to see how they looked. He found a large, sturdy branch he liked. And when evening came and Tabaqui appeared to tell him the council was meeting, Mowgli laughed until the jackal ran away.

At the council, Akela lay next to his rock. It was a sign that the leadership of the pack was open. Shere Kahn paced to and fro, followed by his scrap-fed wolves. Bagheera lay close to Mowgli, who kept the fire-pot between his knees. When all were present, Shere Kahn began to speak.

"He has no right," Bagheera whispered. "Say something."

Mowgli sprang to his feet. "Brothers," he cried, "does Shere Kahn lead the pack? What does a tiger have to do with our leadership?"

"Since the leadership is open, and since I was asked to speak —" Shere Kahn began.

"By whom?" Mowgli asked. "Are we *all* tiger-flattering jackals? The leadership of the pack is to be decided by the pack. You are not one of us."

The wolves spoke out. Some of them wanted the man-cub silenced. Others said he had kept the Law and should be allowed to speak. Finally, the older wolves in the pack said, "Let the Dead Wolf speak."

Dead Wolf is what the wolves call the pack leader from the moment he has missed his kill until he is killed himself, which is usually not long.

Akela raised his weary head. "Fellow wolves — and jackals of Shere Kahn — I have led you for many seasons. In all my time not one of you has been trapped or hurt. Now I have missed my kill. You led me to a strong buck and made my weakness known. It was cleverly done. By the

Law of the Jungle it is your right to kill me here. And it is my right to fight you one by one. Who will step forward?"

There was a long silence. Not one wolf wanted to fight Akela to the death. Then Shere Kahn roared. "What do we care about this toothless fool? It is the man-cub who has lived too long. You should have let me eat him long ago. Give him to me now, or I will hunt here forever and not give you one bone. He is a man! He has no place in the jungle."

More than half the pack took up the cry. "A man! A man! Send him back to live with other men!"

"If we let him go, he will turn the village people against us," Shere Kahn yelled. "He is a man and none of us can look him in the eyes. Give him to me!"

Akela lifted his head again. "He has eaten our food. He has slept with us. He has not broken a single Law of the Jungle."

"And I paid for him with a buffalo. A buffalo may be worth little, but my honor is something that I will fight for," Bagheera added in his gentlest voice.

"The buffalo was paid ten years ago. We do not care about old bones," the young wolves of the pack snarled.

"No man-cub can run with the animals of the jungle," Shere Kahn howled. "Give him to me!"

"He is our brother in all but blood," Akela said gravely, "and yet you would kill him here. Truly, I have lived too long. I see that some of you have become cattle eaters. I have heard that others go with Shere Kahn to snatch children from the villagers' doorsteps. I know you have become cowards, and it is to the cowards that I speak. I know I must die. If my life were worth more, I would give it in Mowgli's place. But for the honor of the pack, I promise you this: If you let the man-cub go to the place of men, I will not bare a tooth against you. I will die without fighting. That will spare the pack at least three lives and the shame of killing a brother who has done nothing wrong."

"He is not our brother — he is a man!" the pack snarled again and again as most of the wolves gathered around Shere Kahn and his switching tail.

"Now it is up to you," Bagheera said to Mowgli. "All *we* can do is fight."

Mowgli stood with the fire-pot in his hands. He stretched out his arms and yawned in the face of the council. Inside he bubbled with rage and sorrow. Until then, he had not known how much the wolves hated him.

"Listen," he cried. "I have heard enough of your dog-jabber. I would have been a wolf with you all my life. But you have told me so many times tonight that I am a man that I finally believe you. No longer can I call you my brothers. I will call you dogs. And because you are dogs and I am a man, *I* will settle this matter. I have here a little Red Flower, which you dogs fear."

Mowgli flung the fire-pot down. A small tuft of moss flared, and the wolves and Shere Kahn drew back in terror before the flames.

Mowgli thrust his branch into the fire until it crackled. Then he whirled it over his head. The wolves cowered.

"You are the master," Bagheera said softly. "Save Akela from death. He has always been your friend."

Standing tall in the light of the blazing branch, Mowgli looked around slowly. The shadows jumped. "I will go to my own people, if they are my own people. The jungle is shut to me. I will forget your talk and your companionship. But I will be more merciful than you. Because I was your brother once, I promise never to betray you to the world of men."

Mowgli kicked the fire with his foot and

sparks flew up. He walked toward Shere Kahn, who sat blinking stupidly at the flames, and grabbed the tiger by the hair on his chin. Bagheera followed closely, in case of accidents.

"Up, dog," Mowgli cried, "or I will set your coat on fire!"

Though he stood, Shere Kahn's ears lay flat and his eyes were shut tight.

"This cattle killer said he would kill me tonight because he had not killed me when I was a cub," Mowgli announced. "Since he insists that I am a man and not a wolf, I will treat him as a man would treat him." Mowgli beat Shere Kahn over the head with the flaming branch. The tiger whimpered and whined in pain and fear.

"Ha! Go now, singed jungle-cat. But remember, when I come back to the Council Rock, it will be with your hide on my head. And as for the rest of you, you will *not* kill Akela because I do not wish it. He will go free and live as his pleases. And if you sit here with your tongues out any longer, I will drive you off like dogs. Go!"

The fire was burning brightly on Mowgli's stick, and he struck right and left around the circle. The wolves ran, howling, as sparks burned their fur. Soon only Akela, Bagheera, and the ten wolves who had taken Mowgli's side were left.

Something inside Mowgli began to hurt. It hurt like nothing he had felt before. He caught his breath and sobbed. Tears ran down his face. "What is it? What is it?" he asked, touching his tears. "I don't want to leave the jungle. I don't know what is happening. Am I dying, Bagheera?"

"No, Little Brother," Bagheera said. "Those are tears. Now I know you are a man and not a cub any longer. The jungle is shut to you, Mowgli. Let them fall. They are only tears."

Mowgli sat and cried as though his

heart would break. "I will go now, but first I must say good-bye to my mother."

He went to the cave where his family lived and cried on Mother Wolf's coat while her four new cubs howled miserably.

"You will not forget me?" Mowgli asked.

"Never. When you miss us, come to the foot of the hill and we will talk to you," Father Wolf said.

"We will play with you in the fields," the young cubs said.

"Come soon," Father Wolf said. "We are getting old, your mother and I."

"Come soon," Mother Wolf said. "Little naked child of man, I loved you more than I loved my own cubs."

"I will come," Mowgli said. "And when I do, it will be to lay Shere Kahn's hide on Council Rock. Do not forget me. Tell - everyone in the jungle never to forget me!"

The dawn was beginning to break when Mowgli went down the hill alone, on his way to meet those mysterious things called men.

Kaa's
Hunting

NOW we go back to the days when Baloo, the old brown bear, was teaching Mowgli the Law of the Jungle. As a man-cub, Mowgli had much to learn, for it was Baloo's goal that he be safe from all creatures in all parts of the jungle. Sometimes Bagheera, the black panther, would creep through the jungle and listen from a tree branch to the lesson of the day, to see how Mowgli was getting along. And so it was today.

For the most part, Mowgli was a wonderful student, and Baloo was pleased to be his teacher. Mowgli could climb almost as well as he could swim and swim almost as well as he could run. Baloo taught him the wood and water laws, such as how to tell a rotten branch from a sturdy one, how to speak nicely to the wild bees when he came upon a hive, what to say to Mang the Bat when he disturbed him at midday, and how to warn the water snakes in the river pools before he splashed down among them. Baloo also taught the boy the Strangers' Hunting Call, which Mowgli was to use whenever he needed to hunt outside his own territory.

Mowgli listened to all that Baloo told him. But sometimes it seemed to him that there was just too much to learn and that Baloo was too stern a teacher. He grew tired of repeating the same Laws over and over. And so, on this day, when Baloo got angry with him, Mowgli ran off altogether.

Baloo sighed and spoke to Bagheera. "A man-cub is a man-cub, and he must learn *all* the Laws of the Jungle, not just the parts that wolf-cubs know."

"But he is so small!" said the panther,

who would have spoiled Mowgli. "How can his little head hold all the Laws you want to put in it?"

"Nothing in the jungle is too small to be killed," Baloo said earnestly. "It is better that he be scolded by me than harmed by another because he does not know the Law. I have been teaching him the Master Words, and if he will only remember them, he will be safe from the birds and the snakes and all that hunt on four feet."

Bagheera stretched out a paw and admired his steel-blue claws. "I am far more likely to be in a position to give help than to ask for it," he said smugly. "But just out of curiosity, what are these Master Words?"

"Let us call Mowgli and have him say them," replied Baloo.

"Come, Little Brother!" Bagheera called aloud.

There was a rustle above them, and a sullen Mowgli slid down the tree trunk. "I come for Bagheera, and not for *thee*, old Baloo!" the boy said with a frown.

"It is all the same to me," Baloo said, though he was actually quite hurt, for he loved the boy a great deal. "Tell Bagheera the Master Words I taught you today."

"Master Words for which people?" Mowgli asked, showing off. "The jungle has many tongues, and I know them all!"

"For the Hunting People," Baloo said.

"We be of one blood, you and I," said Mowgli with a perfect bear accent.

"Well done!" Baloo said. "Now for the birds."

Mowgli spoke the same Master Words in bird-tongue, ending with the kite's whistle.

"And the Snake People," instructed Bagheera.

Mowgli answered with a long hiss, then jumped onto Bagheera's back and drummed his heels on the panther's shiny blue-black coat.

"There!" Baloo said proudly, patting his big stomach. "He is quite safe now, because not beast, bird, nor snake will harm him. No one is to be feared."

"Except his own tribe," Bagheera said under his breath.

"And so I shall have a tribe of my own!" Mowgli said excitedly. "And lead them through the branches all the day long!"

"What is this silliness?" asked Bagheera.

"We shall throw branches and dirt at Baloo," Mowgli went on. "The monkeys have promised me this!"

Whoof! Baloo's giant paw scooped Mowgli off the panther's back.

"Mowgli," said Baloo angrily. "You have been talking with the Bandar-log, the Monkey People, who have no Law. This is a great shame."

Mowgli stole a look at Bagheera, whose eyes were hard as jade.

"They were kind to me when Baloo was too stern," Mowgli replied with a sniffle.

"They came down from the trees and had pity on me when no one else cared. They gave me nuts and good things to eat and carried me to the treetops. They told me I am their blood brother and should be their leader someday."

"They lie," said Bagheera. "They have *no* leader."

"Man-cub," said Baloo, his voice like thunder. "I have taught you the Law of the Jungle for all the creatures of the jungle except the Bandar-log, who live in the trees. This is because they have no Law. They respect nobody. They listen to nobody. They boast that they are a great - people with great plans, but then a nut falls and they forget what they just said and fight among themselves over nothing. We of the jungle have nothing to do with them."

Mowgli stared at Baloo. When the bear stopped talking, the jungle seemed very silent.

"The Monkey People want us to notice them," Baloo went on. "But we do not, even when they torment us and throw nuts and filth on our heads, which they love to do."

No sooner were the words out of his mouth than a shower of nuts, twigs, and dirt rained down upon them. Angry howls echoed from the treetops above.

Baloo and Bagheera led Mowgli away, but the Monkey People followed. They were very pleased with themselves, for Baloo, Bagheera, and Mowgli had noticed them.

As the monkeys followed Mowgli and his friends, one of the Monkey People got an idea. He realized that if Mowgli were in their tribe, he could teach them all sorts of useful things, like how to build huts to protect them from the wind. And so the Monkey People decided to kidnap the man-cub.

Baloo and Bagheera led Mowgli

through the jungle until it was time for the midday nap. By now Mowgli was feeling very ashamed of himself, and, as he settled down between the panther and the bear, he vowed to have nothing more to do with the Monkey People.

The next thing Mowgli knew, he was being pulled upward by hard, strong little hands. Then branches swiped at his face and he was staring down through the trees while Baloo's angry cry filled the jungle and Bagheera bounded up a tree trunk with a low growl, teeth bared.

Howling with glee, the Bandar-log lifted Mowgli higher and higher. They laughed and shouted, "Bagheera has noticed us again! All of the jungle sees we are skillful and cunning!"

Mowgli hung on for dear life. Two of the strongest monkeys held Mowgli by the arms, zooming up and down their roads and crossroads nearly a hundred feet above the ground.

Mowgli tried to enjoy the rush, but mostly he felt sick as he was jerked up and down, forward and backward, and sometimes flung through the air, his heart in his throat. Sometimes he could see for miles over the treetops, then he would be hurled downward and branches would lash across his face.

At first Mowgli was afraid of being dropped. Then he became angry. And finally he began to think. He had to send word back to Bagheera and Baloo, for the monkeys were traveling so fast that his friends would soon be left behind.

Looking up, Mowgli saw Rann the Kite soaring in the air as he waited for his next meal. Rann noticed right away that the monkeys were carrying something, so he swooped in to see what it was and if it was good to eat. When he saw that it was the man-cub, he whistled in surprise.

Mowgli quickly called out the Master Words for birds, as Baloo had taught him.

Rann could see Mowgli's little brown face appearing and disappearing between the branches.

"Mark my trail!" Mowgli said. "And tell Baloo the Bear and Bagheera the Panther!"

"In whose name, Brother?" Rann called. The kite had heard of Mowgli, but had never actually met him.

"Mowgli the Man-cub!" Mowgli shrieked as he was swung through the air.

Rann nodded, then rose higher above the trees and hung in one place, watching the flight of the Bandar-log and their prisoner to see where they were going.

Down in the jungle, Baloo and Bagheera were sick with worry.

"What if they drop him?" Baloo fretted. "What if Mowgli forgets the Master Words? Oh, put dead bats on my head! Give me black bones to eat! I am the most miserable of bears!" He threw himself down on the ground and rocked back and forth, moaning.

"The man-cub is wise and well taught," Bagheera said calmly. "And he has eyes that make the Jungle People afraid. But the Bandar-log fear no one and cannot be trusted."

Suddenly, Baloo sat up. "Hathi the Wild Elephant says, 'To each his own fear.' The Bandar-log fear Kaa the Python. The mere whisper of his name makes their wicked tails cold, for he steals monkeys in the night. And Kaa is always hungry. We shall go to him."

Baloo and Bagheera found Kaa stretched out on a warm rock in the afternoon sun. The giant snake was admiring his new skin, for he had been in seclusion for the past ten days while shedding his old one. Darting his blunt-nosed head along the ground, he twisted and coiled and knotted the thirty feet of his body. Kaa was not a poisonous snake, but he had the power to hypnotize, and his hug was deadly. Each time he licked his lips, he thought of his next meal.

"He has not eaten recently," Baloo said, sounding relieved. "He will be eager to hunt the Bandar-log. But be careful, Bagheera. Kaa is always a little blind after he has changed his skin and is quick to attack."

"Good hunting!" cried Baloo as he approached the snake. Bagheera came up behind Baloo slowly, for he did not know Kaa well and was wary of him.

"Good hunting for us all," Kaa replied. "Is there any news of game afoot? I am as empty as a dried well."

"We are hunting," said Baloo casually. He did not want Kaa to know how much he and Bagheera needed his help.

"Allow me to come with you," Kaa said, "or I shall have to wait for days on a wood path and climb half a night for the chance at a young ape. I came very near to falling on my last hunt, and the noise of my almost-falling waked the Bandar-log. They called me the most evil names."

"Footless, yellow earthworm," murmured Bagheera, putting the name into Kaa's head.

"Did they call me *that*?" Kaa asked with a low hiss.

"Something like that," Bagheera replied. "They will say anything — even that you have lost your teeth and dare not hunt anything bigger than a baby goat, because you are afraid of the ram's horns."

Kaa's black eyes were steady, but Baloo and Bagheera could see the muscles on his throat ripple and bulge with anger.

"It is the Bandar-log that we follow now," said Baloo.

"Those nut stealers and pickers of palm leaves have stolen our man-cub," Bagheera added. "Have you heard of him?"

"I heard news from Ikki the Porcupine of a manling that was part of the wolf-pack. But Ikki is full of stories that are half heard and badly told. I did not believe."

"It is true," said Baloo. "He is the best and wisest and boldest of man-cubs. I — we — love him, Kaa."

"Our man-cub is in the treacherous little hands of the Bandar-log, who fear Kaa alone," said Bagheera.

"They have good reason to fear me," said Kaa. "Chattering, foolish, vain creatures. We must remind them to speak well of their master. Where have they taken the manling?"

"Toward the sunset, I believe," said Baloo. "Though the jungle alone knows."

Just then a cry came from above. "Up, up! *Hillo! Illo!* Look up, Baloo!" Rann the Kite was soaring overhead, the sun shining on the edges of his wings. "I have seen Mowgli among the Bandar-log, and he asked me to tell you. They have taken him to Monkey City, the Cold Lairs. That is my message."

"A filling meal and a deep sleep I wish for you, Rann!" cried Bagheera. "I will remember your deed and set aside part of my next kill for you."

"It is nothing," Rann replied as he circled to leave. "The boy spoke the Master Words."

"He has not forgotten to use his tongue or his teaching," Baloo said with a chuckle of pride.

"I am proud of him," agreed Bagheera. "But now we must go to the Cold Lairs."

The Cold Lairs was a place that all the Jungle People knew of but seldom visited. An old deserted city, lost and buried in the jungle, it had once been inhabited by man. Only the monkeys spent time there now.

"It is half a night's journey," Bagheera said, looking at Baloo.

"I will go as fast as I can," replied the bear.

"Kaa and I must go ahead," said

Bagheera. "Follow us as quickly as you can." The panther rushed ahead at a fast canter, while a silent Kaa kept up easily.

"You are no slow-goer, Kaa," remarked Bagheera.

"I am hungry," Kaa replied, finding the shortest route and slithering along beside him. "And they called me names."

In the Cold Lairs, the Monkey People were very pleased with themselves for capturing the man-cub. And Mowgli, who had never seen a man-made city before, was fascinated by the decrepit buildings all around him. The ruin was set on a little hill. Trees had grown into and out of the walls of the houses, and wild vines hung out of the tower windows of the crumbling palace of a long-dead king. The cobblestones in the courtyard where the king's elephants once stood were now thrust apart by wild grasses and young trees. Below the palace were the rows and rows of roofless houses that made

up the city, as dark and empty as cata-
combs.

The monkeys called the ruins Monkey
City and pretended to be men. But they
had no idea what the structures were or
how to use them. They explored all the
rooms and buildings but never remembered what they had seen. They sat in the
king's council chamber and scratched for
fleas or ran in and out of the roofless
houses collecting broken bricks or plaster.
But they always forgot where they hid the
bricks and plaster and would fight
among themselves about it. Then they
would run down to the palace terrace and
shake the orange trees, just to watch the
fruit fall.

Over and over again the Monkey People did these things in Monkey City, until
they grew bored and went back to the jungle treetops, hoping that the Jungle People would finally notice them.

Mowgli did not understand or like the

way the monkeys lived, for he had grown up with the Law of the Jungle and the Bandar-log had no Laws. They did not let him rest after their long journey and did not give him anything to eat.

"Mowgli will teach us how to weave sticks together to protect us from the cold," one of the monkeys told his companions. But when Mowgli showed them how to do this, they imitated him for only a minute before losing interest, howling, and pulling one another's tails.

"I want to eat," said Mowgli. "Bring me food, or give me permission to hunt here."

Several monkeys bounded away to bring him food, but they got into a fight out on the road and left the nuts and fruits they'd gathered lying in the dust. Frustrated, Mowgli roamed the city, giving the Strangers' Hunting Call. But nobody answered him, and he began to feel lonely and afraid.

"Everything Baloo told me about the

Monkey People is true," Mowgli said to himself. "I must try to get back to my own part of the jungle."

But as soon as Mowgli walked to the edge of the city, the monkeys dragged him back, telling him how lucky he was to be with them, the great Bandar-log. They led him to a terrace above the sandstone reservoirs, which were half full of water. The terrace was lovely, with a summerhouse whose walls were made of beautifully carved marble set with colorful, polished stones. As darkness fell, the moonlight shone through the carvings and cast delicate shadows on the ground.

Hundreds of monkeys gathered on the terrace to tell stories about how strong and brave and wise they were. The tales went on and on, and whenever a speaker paused, all the monkeys would shout, "We are the most wonderful people in all the jungle! We all say so, and it must be true!"

Mowgli was exhausted, and his head

spun with the noise of the monkeys' voices. "Tabaqui the Jackal must have bitten all these people," he told himself, "and now they are all crazy."

Mowgli looked up and saw a large cloud about to cover the moon. "I should try to run away in the darkness of the cloud cover," he told himself. "But I am so tired."

In the ditch below the city wall, two other creatures watched the same cloud and the mass of monkeys. They, too, were waiting for darkness. Even a panther and a python were no match for two hundred Bandar-log.

"I will go to the west wall and come down swiftly, with the slope in my favor," said Kaa as the cloud hid the moon.

"I wish Baloo were here," said Bagheera, "but we must do what we can without him."

Up on the terrace, Mowgli heard the sound of Bagheera's feet behind him as the panther broke the circle of monkeys surrounding the man-cub.

"There is only one here! Kill him!" shouted one of the monkeys. In an instant, a scuffling mass of monkeys attacked Bagheera, biting, tearing, and scratching his body. Half a dozen others grabbed Mowgli and carried him up a wall of the summerhouse, dropping him through a hole in the domed ceiling. Mowgli was trapped.

"Stay there until we have killed your friend," the monkeys chattered. "Later we will play with you, if the snakes dwelling here haven't killed you first."

Mowgli wasted no time giving the Snake's call. "We be of one blood, you and I," he said in a long hiss.

"Lower your hoods," replied the dozens of cobras living in the house. The cobras relaxed then, and let their hoods drop down. They would not attack Mowgli.

"But stand still, Little Brother, or you will crush us with your feet."

Mowgli stood still and quiet, peering through the open carvings of the summerhouse. The fight around Bagheera was awful and furious, and the black panther bucked and twisted under the throng of monkeys. For the first time since he was born, Bagheera was fighting for his life.

Mowgli was full of worry and remorse and desperately wanted to help his friend. "Roll to the water tanks and plunge in!" Mowgli called, for he knew that the monkeys would not follow the panther into the water.

Bagheera was exhausted and badly cut, but the sound of little Mowgli's voice filled him with hope. He began to inch his way - toward the reservoir, fighting off the long-armed creatures as he did so.

Then, from behind the city wall rose the rumbling war cry of Baloo. Slipping and sliding up the terrace, he grabbed as many monkeys as he could and batted them hard with his paws.

Splash! Bagheera had made it to the water tank and was, for the moment, safe. A hoard of monkeys leaped and shouted furiously on the terrace nearby, but they did not go in the water. Mang the Bat carried the news of the battle over the jungle until Hathi the Wild Elephant trumpeted, alerting everyone for miles.

Finally, Kaa slithered straight into the mass of monkeys, anxious to do battle. Driving forward with his flat head, he lunged with the strength of a locomotive.

"Kaa! It is Kaa! Run!" shouted the monkeys in fear. Generations of stories had taught them to be deathly afraid of the monstrous python. To them, Kaa was a terrifying creature who could slip along the branches as quietly as moss grows, steal off with the strongest monkey that ever lived, or make himself look so much like a rotten stump that even the wisest monkey was deceived until he was caught and strangled.

Kaa brought fear into the monkeys' hearts because none of them knew the limits of his power, none could look him in the eye, and none had ever survived his hug. Stammering with terror, they ran to the walls and roofs of the long-deserted houses.

Baloo heaved a sigh of relief as Bagheera climbed out of the water tank, shaking himself off. Mowgli did a little dance inside the summerhouse (being careful not to trample the snakes) and hooted like an owl. In the trees and houses, the monkeys shrieked in fear. But when Kaa let out a long *hissss*, the Bandar-log were silenced.

"I think they have pulled me into a hundred little bearlings," Baloo said gravely as he shook out his legs. "Kaa, we owe you our lives, I think."

"No matter," Kaa replied. "Where is the manling?"

"I am trapped in here," Mowgli cried from inside the summerhouse. "I can't climb out." Indeed, the curve of the broken dome was far above his head.

Kaa eyed the wall of the summerhouse carefully, searching for a crack. He tapped the weak spot lightly with his head. Lifting six feet of his body off the ground, he lunged forward with several massive blows, using his nose to break the carved screenwork, which fell to the ground in a cloud of dust and rubble.

Mowgli flung himself at Baloo and Bagheera, throwing an arm around each large neck.

"Are you hurt?" asked Baloo, hugging him tenderly.

"I am sore, hungry, and bruised. But they have hurt both of *you*!"

"It is nothing if you are safe," Baloo said.

"We shall discuss that later," said Bagheera in a serious voice. "Now, Mowgli, you must thank Kaa according to our customs."

Mowgli turned to the giant snake. "We be of one blood, you and I," he said. "I take my life from you tonight. My meal shall be your meal if ever you are hungry, O Kaa."

"All thanks, Little Brother," said Kaa, his eyes twinkling. He was not sure that Mowgli could offer him enough food to fill his long belly, but he was impressed with the boy's courage. "Your brave heart and courteous tongue shall carry you far in the jungle, manling. But now you should leave quickly with your friends, for the moon is setting, and you should not see what is about to happen."

Above them the moon was sinking behind the hills and the shadows of the trembling monkeys looked ragged and fringed. Kaa glided to the center of the terrace and snapped his jaw together, forcing the monkeys to look at him.

"Now begins Kaa's Dance of the Hunger," he said to the monkeys. "Sit still and watch, all of you."

Kaa began to move, weaving his head from left to right as he made circles on the terrace. Then he made loops and figure eights with his long body, and oozy triangles that melted into squares and five-sided figures, and coiled himself into mounds. Never pausing or changing his pace, and singing a low, humming song, he danced until the moonlight disappeared.

Beside Mowgli, Bagheera and Baloo stood still as stones, growling in their throats. Their neck hair stood on end.

"Bandar-log!" Kaa shouted. "Can you move without my order?"

"We cannot, O Kaa!" the monkeys replied together. Indeed, they had been hypnotized by the python's dance.

"Good," said Kaa. "You must all come one step closer to me."

The monkeys followed Kaa's order, as did Baloo and Bagheera. Mowgli reached up and pulled his friends back. As soon as he touched them, the panther and the bear started as if waking from a deep sleep.

"Closer!" Kaa ordered the monkeys. The Bandar-log stepped forward again.

"Keep your hand on my shoulder," said Bagheera with a shiver. "Or I will have to do as the snake says."

"It is only Kaa making circles in the dust," Mowgli said as the three slipped away into the jungle. As a man-cub, he had not been lured by the Dance. "And his nose was all sore."

"His nose was sore because of *you*," Bagheera reminded him, "as my ears and sides and paws and Baloo's neck and shoulders are bitten. You have cost us heavily in time, wounds, and hair — and

68

most importantly, honor. Baloo and I had to call upon Kaa for help, and we were both made foolish by Kaa's Hunger Dance. All of this came, Mowgli, from your playing with the Bandar-log."

"It is all true," said Mowgli sorrowfully. "I did wrong, and both of you are wounded. I know that the Law of the Jungle says I must be punished."

Bagheera raised a paw and gave Mowgli half a dozen love taps, which would have hardly awoken a young panther but were serious blows for a young boy. But when it was over, it was over, and Mowgli jumped onto the panther's back and returned to his own jungle, sleeping soundly the whole way.

Tiger!
Tiger!

NOW we go back to the first tale. When Mowgli left the jungle after his fight with the wolves at Council Rock, he went down to the village at the foot of the hill. But he did not stop there. It was too close to the jungle. He hurried on down the rough road for nearly twenty miles, until he came to a place where he had never been. He stood in a valley that opened on to a plain cut up by deep streams. At one end was a village and at the other end the thick jungle came down to touch the grounds where the cattle were grazing.

When the boys in charge of the herds saw Mowgli, they shouted and ran away. The yellow dogs that hang about every Indian village barked. Mowgli kept walking. He walked right up to the village gate. To one side, Mowgli saw the big thornbush that would be placed in front of the gate at twilight.

"So men are afraid of the Jungle People," Mowgli said to himself. He sat down by the gate and, when a man came by, Mowgli opened his mouth and pointed into it to show that he wanted food.

The man stared and ran up the village street, shouting for the priest. Then the priest, who was a big, fat man dressed in white, with a red and yellow mark on his forehead, came down to the gate with at least a hundred people behind him. Everyone stared and talked and shouted at Mowgli. Mowgli did not know what they were saying, for he had never learned the language of man.

"They have no manners," Mowgli said to himself. "Only the gray ape would behave like this." He frowned at the crowd.

74

"There is nothing to be afraid of," the priest announced. "Look at the marks on his arms and legs. They are wolf bites. He is nothing but a wolf-child run away from the jungle."

Mowgli's limbs were covered in little white scars where the cubs had nipped him harder than they meant to when they played together. But Mowgli would never have called them bites, for he knew what a real bite was.

Two or three of the women cried out, "Poor child! Bitten by wolves! He is a handsome boy. Messua, doesn't he look like your boy? The one that was taken by the tiger?"

"Let me look," said a woman with heavy copper rings on her wrists and ankles. She peered at Mowgli beneath her palm. "He is thinner," she said. "But he has the look of my boy."

The clever priest knew Messua had a rich husband who could afford to take in the boy. So he looked up at the sky for a moment and said solemnly, "What the jungle has taken, the jungle has restored. Sister, take the boy to your house."

"By the buffalo that bought me," Mowgli said to himself, "all of this talk is like the looking-over of the pack! But if I am truly a man, a man I must become." He followed the beckoning woman to her hut.

Messua gave Mowgli a long drink of milk and some bread. Then she looked into his eyes. She thought he might truly be her son. "Nathoo! Nathoo!" she called him. "Do you remember when I gave you your first shoes?" She touched his feet. The bottoms were as hard as horn. And Mowgli did not show any sign of remembering. "No." Messua sighed. "These feet have never worn shoes. But you are like my Nathoo, and you will be my son."

Mowgli felt uneasy. He had never been

under a roof before. But when he looked closer, he saw that he could tear the thatch away if he needed to escape.

"What good is a man if he doesn't understand men's talk?" Mowgli thought. "I must learn to speak like the people of the village." So as soon as Messua pronounced a word, Mowgli imitated it almost perfectly. Before dark he had learned the names of many things in the hut.

Bedtime was difficult. Mowgli did not want to sleep under anything that looked like a panther trap. When Mowgli's new parents shut the door, Mowgli went out the window.

"Let him go," said Messua's husband. "He has never slept in a bed before. And if he is truly our son, he will not run away."

Mowgli stretched out in some clean grass on the edge of the field, but before he had closed his eyes, a soft gray nose poked him under the chin.

"Phew!" said Gray Brother, the oldest of Mother Wolf's cubs. "Little Brother, you smell of woodsmoke and cattle — like a man! This is the reward I get for following you twenty miles?"

Mowgli hugged the wolf. "Are all well in the jungle?" he asked.

"All except the wolves burned by the Red Flower. And Shere Kahn. He has gone to hunt far away until his coat grows back. But listen, he has promised that when he returns, he will lay your bones in the Waingunga River," Gray Brother said.

"I have made a promise myself," Mowgli replied. "Tonight I am tired from so many new things, but it is good to have news. Gray Brother, will you always bring me the news?"

"Will you forget you are a wolf?" Gray Brother asked anxiously.

"Never. I will always remember that I love you and the others that grew up in our cave," Mowgli answered. "But I will also remember that I have been cast out of the pack."

"You may be cast out of another pack. Men are only men, Little Brother," Gray Wolf said. "When I come next, I will wait in the bamboo at the edge of the grazing ground."

For three months, Mowgli hardly left the village gate. He was busy learning the ways of men. He had to wear a cloth around his waist, which annoyed him terribly. He had to learn about money, which he did not understand at all. He also learned to plow the field, which he thought was useless.

The other children in the village were not always nice to Mowgli. Luckily, the Law of the Jungle had taught him to keep his temper. That, and the knowledge that it was unsportsmanlike to kill naked cubs, kept him from hurting the village children when they made fun of him. Mowgli could have caused a lot of damage. In the jungle he was weak compared to the beasts, but in the village Mowgli was said to be as strong as a buffalo.

Many of the village rules confused Mowgli. He did not understand the strange customs of men, so he made many mistakes. To keep Mowgli out of trouble, the priest recommended that he be sent to work as soon as possible. When the village headman assigned Mowgli to take the buffalo to graze the next day, no one was happier than Mowgli.

The night he was appointed to be a herder, Mowgli went to the village circle. The men of the village met under a great fig tree to smoke and gossip. The headman and the barber and old Buldeo, the village hunter, were gathered there, along with many others. They sat around late into the night telling wonderful tales of gods and men and ghosts. Above them, the monkeys in the trees listened. Below them, under a platform, a sacred cobra lay curled up with a plate of milk.

Old Buldeo told the best tales. When he spoke of the ways of the jungle beasts, the eyes of the children listening just outside the circle bulged out of their heads.

Naturally, Mowgli knew more about the beasts than Buldeo. As Buldeo spoke, Mowgli had to cover his face so the villagers wouldn't see him laughing.

Buldeo told everyone that the tiger who took Messua's son was really a ghost tiger, whose body was inhabited by the spirit of a long-dead moneylender. "I know it is true because the tiger walked with a limp, just as Purun Dass did. He got the limp in a riot when his accounting books were burned."

The graybeards nodded together. "True. True," they said.

Mowgli's shoulders shook with laughter. "Are all of these tales such nonsense?" he said. "Everyone knows that Shere Kahn was born lame."

For a moment Buldeo was speechless. "Oho! If you are so smart, perhaps you should bring the tiger's hide to Khanhi-wara. The government has promised a hundred rupees for it. Better yet, jungle brat, do not speak when your elders are talking!"

Mowgli's laughter turned to anger. He did not·like to be scolded, and he stalked off.

"It is high time that boy went herding," the headman said as Mowgli walked away from the circle.

The next morning Mowgli rode through the village on the back of Rama, the great herd bull. The buffalo rose up from their mangers, one by one, to follow him.

In most Indian villages it is the job of a few young boys to take the domestic cattle and water buffalo out to graze in the morning and bring them back at night. As long as the boys stay with the herds, they are safe, for not even a tiger will charge a mob of cattle.

Mowgli quickly made it clear to the other children tending the herds that he was in charge. He told the other boys to graze the cattle while he went on with the buffalo. Then he drove the buffalo to the edge of the jungle, dropped off Rama's neck, and trotted over to a clump of bamboo.

"I have been waiting for days!" Gray Brother said, emerging from the foliage. "What are you doing herding?"

"It is an order. I am working for the village," Mowgli replied impatiently. "Now tell me about Shere Kahn."

"He came back and waited for you for a long time," Gray Brother said. "But now he is gone again because food is scarce. Still, he intends to kill you."

"Good," said Mowgli. "As long as he is away, I want you or one of your brothers to sit upon that rock, so I can see you as I ride out of the village. When he returns, wait for me in the ravine, by the great tree in the center of the plain. I will not walk into Shere Kahn's mouth!"

Then Mowgli lay down in a shady spot and slept while the buffalo grazed and wallowed in the mud.

Day after day Mowgli led the buffalo out to their mud wallows. Day after day he saw Gray Brother's back way across the plain and knew Shere Kahn had not returned. And day after day Mowgli lay in the grass listening to the noises around him, dreaming of the jungle.

At last the day came when Mowgli did not see Gray Brother at the signal spot. Quickly, he herded the buffalo up the ravine to the great tree in the center of the plain. There sat Gray Brother with every bristle on his back standing up. "Shere Kahn hid for a month to catch you off guard. He crossed the ranges with

Tabaqui last night. He is hot on your trail," the wolf said, panting.

Mowgli frowned. "I am not afraid of Shere Kahn, but Tabaqui is very clever."

"Have no fear," Gray Brother said, licking his lips. "I met Tabaqui at dawn. He is telling his story to the scavenging kites now, but before I broke his back he told *me* everything.

"Shere Kahn is planning to wait for you tonight at the village gate — you and you alone. He is hiding now in the dry river ravine of the Waingunga," Gray Brother reported.

"Has he eaten today, or does he hunt empty?" Mowgli knew the answer meant life or death to him.

"He killed at dawn — a pig — and he has drunk, too," Gray Brother said. "Shere Kahn could never go hungry, even for the sake of revenge."

"Oh, what a fool!" Mowgli nearly laughed. "He has eaten and drunk and thinks I will wait until he has slept! No, together with the buffalo, we will take him by surprise. The buffalo will not charge unless they catch wind of him, and I cannot speak their language. Can we get behind the tiger's track so they can smell it?"

"Shere Kahn swam far down the Waingunga to hide his scent," said Gray Brother.

"Tabaqui must have told him to do that. He would not have thought of it himself." Mowgli stood with his finger in his mouth, thinking. "The big ravine of the Waingunga opens onto the plain a half mile from here. I can take the herd through the jungle to the head of the ravine — but he would slink out at the foot. We need to block the other end. Gray Brother, can you cut the herd in two for me?"

"Not by myself," Gray Brother said. "But I have brought a wise helper." A great gray head lifted up from a nearby hole in the ground. It was a head Mowgli knew well.

"Akela! Akela!" Mowgli clapped his hands. "I knew you would not forget me! We have work to do, Akela. Cut the herd in two — keep the buffalo cows and calves together, and the bulls by themselves."

Akela and Gray Brother ran in and out of the herd, separating it into two clumps. The cows circled their calves. They glared and pawed the ground, ready to charge if one of the wolves stayed still long enough. In the other group, the bulls snorted and stamped. Alhough they looked more imposing than the cows, they were far less dangerous, because they had no calves to protect.

"What now?" Akela asked.

Mowgli slipped onto Rama's back. "Drive the bulls away to the left, Akela. Gray Brother, keep the cows together and drive them to the foot of the ravine."

"How far?" Gray Brother asked, panting and snapping to keep the clumps of buffalo separate.

"Drive them until the sides of the ravine are higher than Shere Kahn can jump," Mowgli shouted. "Keep them there until we come down!"

While Gray Brother led the cows to the ravine, Akela turned the bulls toward the jungle.

"Turn them swiftly," Mowgli called. "Careful, Akela. One snap too many and the bulls will charge. Rama is mad with rage. I wish that I could tell him what I need from him today!"

The bulls crashed into the thicket. The other children, watching the cattle a half mile away, saw what was happening and hurried to the village as fast as their legs - could carry them. They shouted that the buffalo had gone mad and run away.

Mowgli's plan was simple. He wanted to circle the bulls around to the head of the ravine, to catch Shere Kahn between the bulls and the cows. He knew that after a meal and drink, Shere Kahn would be in no condition to fight or clamber up the sides of the ravine.

Using his voice, Mowgli soothed the bulls in front as they went. Akcla dropped back, only whimpering when he wanted to hurry the bulls at the rear. They made a wide circle, so Shere Kahn would not hear them coming. When at last they reached the head of the ravine, Mowgli looked with satisfaction at the steep sides. They rose nearly straight up, and the creepers and vines that grew on them would give no foothold to a tiger trying to climb out.

"Let them breathe," Mowgli instructed Akela. "The bulls have not caught wind of Shere Kahn yet. I can tell him we are coming — he is already in our trap." Mowgli put his hands to his mouth. His shouts echoed down the ravine, jumping from rock to rock.

After a long time, they heard a reply — the drawling, sleepy snarl of a full tiger waking up.

"Who calls?" Shere Kahn whined.

"It is I, Mowgli. Cattle thief, it is time to come to the Council Rock!" Mowgli turned to look at his old pack leader. "*Now*, Akela. Hurry them down. Down, Rama, down!" he said to the bull.

The herd paused for an instant at the edge of the slope, then one by one charged over it, sand and stones flying up around them. Once the herd started running, there was no stopping it. As they reached the bed of the ravine, Rama caught Shere Kahn's scent and bellowed.

"Now you know," Mowgli said from Rama's back.

A storm of black horns, foaming muzzles, and staring eyes whirled down the ravine. The terrible charge of the buffalo herd was something no tiger could hope to survive.

When Shere Kahn heard the thunder of hooves, he picked himself up and lumbered away. He looked from side to side for an escape, but the walls of the ravine were too straight. Heavy with food and drink, he kept running. He was willing to do anything to avoid a fight.

The herd splashed through the pool Shere Kahn had just left. The ravine rang with their bellows. And then came an answering bellow from the foot of the ravine. Mowgli heard the cows call. He saw Shere Kahn turn, choosing to face the bulls instead of the cows. As the bulls rushed toward the tiger, Mowgli felt Rama trip, stumble on something soft, and race on.

The herds crashed full into one another and the force drove them both out onto the plain, stamping and snorting Mowgli waited until the right moment, then slipped off Rama, tapping him with his stick. "Quick, Akela," he called.

"Break them up so they will not hurt each other."

Akela and Gray Brother ran to and fro, nipping legs. "Softly, now, softly. It is all over," Mowgli called to the herd until at last they were calm and he could lead them to the mud pools.

Back in the ravine, Shere Kahn was dead and the kites were coming for him already.

"Brothers, that was a dog's death," Mowgli said, reaching for the knife he carried now that he lived with men. "But he would not have put up a good fight. His hide will look good on the Council Rock. We must work quickly."

A boy trained among men would never have dreamed of skinning a ten-foot tiger alone. It was hard work, even with the help of the wolves, tugging with him when he asked.

After a while, Mowgli felt a hand on his shoulder. He looked up to see Buldeo, the village hunter. The children had told him about the buffalo stampede, and Buldeo had taken his gun and set out angrily, anxious to scold Mowgli for not taking better care of the herd. The wolves dropped out of sight as soon as they saw a man coming.

"What is this foolishness?" Buldeo roared. "You think you can skin a tiger? " He looked more closely at the body of Shere Khan. "It is the lame tiger with one hundred rupees on his head. Well, perhaps we will overlook your letting the herd run off. I might even give you one rupee after we take the skin to Khanhiwara."

"You will take the hide and give me one rupee? Ha!" Mowgli snorted. "*I* will take the skin for my own use, old man."

"How dare you talk like that to the chief hunter of the village!" Buldeo shouted. "Your luck and the stupidity of the buffalo helped you kill this tiger. You can't even skin him properly, little beggar-brat. I will not give you one anna of the reward. Leave the carcass!"

"By the buffalo that bought me," Mowgli said as he struggled on with his work, "must I talk to this old ape all afternoon? Here, Akela, this man is bothering me."

Buldeo, who was stooping by Shere Kahn's head, suddenly found himself sprawling on the grass with a gray wolf standing over him.

"You are right, Buldeo," Mowgli said, gritting his teeth. "You will not give me one anna of the reward. There is an old war between this lame tiger and me — a very old war. And I have won."

If Buldeo had been ten years younger, he would have taken his chances fighting Akela . . . if they had met in the woods. But a wolf in the woods is not the same as a wolf that takes orders from a boy who has private wars with man-eating tigers!

Buldeo was sure that this was some sort of sorcery. He lay as still as he could, expecting Mowgli to turn into a tiger at any moment.

"Maharaj! Great King!" Buldeo said at last in a husky whisper.

Mowgli chuckled and did not bother to turn his head. "Yes?"

"I am an old man," Buldeo whispered. "I did not know you were anything more than a herd boy. Please, may I rise and go, or will your servant tear me to pieces?"

"Go, and peace go with you," Mowgli answered. "But next time, do not meddle with my game. Let him go, Akela."

Akela stepped back and Buldeo hobbled off as fast as he could. Several times he looked back over his shoulder to see if Mowgli had turned into anything terrible. When he reached the village, he told wild tales of enchantment and sorcery.

It was twilight when Mowgli finished

his work. He left the tiger's skin with Gray Brother to guard it. "Now we must take the buffalo home," he said. "Help me herd them, Akela."

As the herd neared the misty village, Mowgli saw lights. The sound of shouting, banging, and bells filled the air. Half the village waited by the gate. Mowgli thought they were celebrating because he had killed Shere Kahn. But as he drew closer, stones whistled past his ears and the villagers shouted: "Wolf's brat!" "Sorcerer!" "Jungle demon!" "Go away!" "Shoot him, Buldeo!"

Buldeo's gun went off with a bang, and a young buffalo bellowed in pain.

"It's more sorcery," the villagers shouted. "He can turn bullets! Buldeo, that was *your* buffalo."

Mowgli did not understand what was happening. The stones kept flying.

"They are like the pack, these new brothers of yours," Akela said, sitting calmly by. "I think they are trying to cast you out."

"Wolf! Wolf's cub! Go away!" The priest shouted and waved a stick.

"Again?" Mowgli asked. "Last time it was because I was a man, this time it is because I am a wolf. Let's go, Akela."

Suddenly, Messua ran toward him. "Oh, my son! My son!" she cried. "They say you are a sorcerer and you can turn yourself into a beast. I do not believe it, but please, go away or they will kill you. I know you have avenged Nathoo's death."

"Come back, Messua, or we will throw stones at you, too," the villagers shouted.

Mowgli started to laugh, but it was cut short by a stone that hit him in the mouth. "Go back, Messua. This is only one of the foolish tales they will tell under the tree at dusk. I have paid for your son's life, but go now, quickly. I will send the herd in more swiftly than their stones. Now, once more, Akela!" Mowgli cried.

The buffalo were anxious to go home. They did not need Akela to convince them. They charged the gate at full speed, scattering the crowd.

"Keep count," Mowgli shouted. "I may have stolen one of them. Keep count, for I shall do your herding no more. Farewell, children of men. Be thankful to Messua. It is for her sake that I will not come with my wolves to hunt you in your streets."

Mowgli turned on his heel and walked away with Akela by his side. As he walked, he looked up at the stars and felt happy. "No more sleeping in traps for me," he said. "Come, let's get Shere Kahn's skin and go."

As the moon rose, the villagers watched Mowgli trot across the plain with two wolves at his heels and a bundle on his head. They banged the temple bells and blew conches as loudly as they could. Messua cried, and Buldeo told the story, embellishing it more and more. In the end, he finished it by saying that Akela had stood up on his hind legs and spoken like a man.

The moon was just going down when Mowgli and the two wolves came to Mother Wolf's cave. "They have cast me out of the man-pack, Mother," Mowgli said. "But I have returned with the hide of Shere Kahn, to keep my word."

Mother Wolf walked out of the cave with her four youngest cubs behind her. Her eyes glowed when she saw the tiger's skin. "I told him on the day he shoved his head into our cave that the hunter would become the hunted. Well done, Little Frog."

"Well done, Little Brother," said a deep voice in the thicket. "We have been lonely in the jungle without you." Bagheera came running and stood by Mowgli's bare feet. Then, together, they climbed up to Council Rock.

Mowgli spread the skin on the stone

where Akela used to sit and held it fast with bamboo slivers. Akela lay down upon it and called to the council, "Look! Look well, O wolves!" exactly as he had done when Mowgli was first brought there.

Although the pack had been without a leader since Mowgli left, they answered Akela's call. Without a leader, they had been left to hunt on their own. Some were lame from traps and some limped from wounds. Others were mangy from eating bad food. Many were missing. All that were left answered the call and saw Shere Kahn's striped hide on the rock, with its huge claws dangling down.

Then Mowgli began to sing. It was a song without any rhymes that came into his throat all by itself. He shouted it aloud, leaping up and down on the skin until he was out of breath. Gray Brother and Akela howled between the verses.

"Look well, O wolves. Have I kept my

word?" Mowgli asked when he was finished.

"Yes," the wolves bayed.

Then a tattered-looking wolf howled. "Lead us again, Akela. Lead us, man-cub. We want to be a pack once more."

"No," Bagheera purred. "When your bellies are full, you may go mad again. You fought for this freedom and now it is yours. Eat it, O wolves."

"Man-pack and wolf-pack have cast me out," Mowgli said. "Now I will hunt alone in the jungle."

"We will hunt with you," said the four wolves Mowgli had grown up with.

From that day on, Mowgli hunted in the jungle, but Mowgli was not always alone: Years later he became a man and married. But that is a story for grown-ups.

Rikki-tikki-tavi

RIKKI-tikki-tavi was a brave and clever mongoose who fought a great battle against two conniving cobras living in the gardens of the big bungalow in Segowlee, India. Although he had help from Darzee, the tailorbird, and Chuchundra, the muskrat, Rikki did all of the real fighting himself.

Rikki had a fluffy bottlebrush tail and a restless pink nose. His eyes were pink, too, except when he was angry. When Rikki was angry, his eyes glowed a fiery red. And as he scuttled quickly through the long grasses, he uttered a mischievous sound that mimicked his name: *Rikk-tikk-tikki-tikki-tchk!*

Rikki did not always live in the big bungalow. Like most young mongooses, he grew up with his mother and father in a cozy burrow. But one day a great flood washed him out of his home and sent him kicking and sputtering down a roadside ditch. The next thing he knew, he was lying in the middle of a garden path and a small boy was standing over him saying, "Look, it's a dead mongoose. Let's bury him and have a funeral."

The little boy's mother peered at the young mongoose. "Perhaps he isn't dead at all," she said. "Let's take him into the house and dry him off."

Rikki, of course, was *not* dead. As soon as he had been dried and warmed, he sat up, wiggled his nose, and looked around. Then he scratched himself, put his fur in order, and jumped onto the boy's shoulder.

"He's tickling under my chin!" cried the boy, whose name was Teddy.

Teddy's parents laughed. "Let's give him something to eat," suggested Teddy's father.

Rikki rubbed his nose against Teddy's ear, then climbed down to the floor. After a delicious snack of raw meat, he busied himself exploring the house. Curious about everything, he nearly fell into the bathtub, got his nose covered in ink from the inkwell, and burned his whiskers on the end of Teddy's father's cigar when he climbed onto his shoulder to see how writing was done. Rikki was truly enjoying himself.

The next morning Rikki dined on boiled egg and banana, scampering from one lap to another between bites. He was thrilled with his new family, for every young mongoose hopes to be a house mongoose when he grows up, and Rikki was no exception.

His belly half full (a full belly makes for a slow mongoose), Rikki went out to explore the garden. Dashing among the tall grasses, citrus trees, rosebushes, and bamboos, he licked his lips. This was fertile hunting ground indeed! Fluffing up his tail, Rikki heard a mournful cry coming from the thornbush.

Darzee, the tailorbird, and his wife were weeping.

"What is the matter?" asked Rikki, his nose quivering.

"We are very miserable," replied Darzee. "One of our babies fell out of the nest and Nag ate him!"

"That is very sad," agreed Rikki. "But who is Nag?"

Just at that moment a low hiss came from the thick grass nearby, making Rikki shiver and jump back. Then, inch by inch, the head and hood of a large black cobra rose into the air.

"I am Nag," hissed the cobra, his wicked black eyes staring at Rikki. "Look, and be afraid!"

Rikki stared at the giant snake but only felt fear for a moment, because a mongoose is never afraid for long. Rikki had never met a cobra before, but his mother had fed him on dead ones, and he knew it was a grown mongoose's work to kill and eat snakes. And though his staring black eyes did not show what he was feeling, Nag knew this to be true, too, and his cold heart was full of fear.

Rikki's tail fluffed up. "Well, do you think it is right to eat young birds who have fallen from their nest?"

Nag didn't answer but watched the grass behind Rikki flicker. He knew that a mongoose in the garden meant death for his family sooner or later, and he wanted to distract this newcomer.

"Let us talk," Nag said smoothly. "You eat eggs. Why shouldn't I eat birds?"

"Look out!" cried Darzee. "Behind you!"

Rikki needed no prodding. As soon as

the words were out of Darzee's mouth, he leaped into the air as high as he could.

Hissssssssss! Beneath him, the hooded head of Nagaina, Nag's wicked wife, whizzed by. Rikki came down and bit Nagaina's back, but he did not hold on long enough to kill her because he was startled by the way she lashed violently about.

"Wicked Darzee!" cried Nag angrily as Rikki leaped to safety. The mongoose's eyes were glowing red and his teeth chattered with rage. While Nag and Nagaina slithered away into the grass, Rikki trotted off to the gravel garden path and sat down to think. These cobras were something to contend with. But on the other hand, Rikki was pleased with himself, for a young mongoose rarely survives an attack from behind. And so, when Teddy appeared a few minutes later, Rikki was ready to be petted.

As Teddy ran toward Rikki, a tiny voice called out from the dust: "Be careful, I am death!" It was Karait, a small brown snakeling with a bite as deadly as the cobra's.

At once Rikki's eyes glowed red again and he danced up to Karait, rocking back and forth and looking for a good place to bite the tiny creature. If Rikki had known just how dangerous the small snake's poison could be, he might have been more cautious. But Rikki did not know.

"Look!" Teddy called to his parents. "Our mongoose is fighting a snake!"

Teddy's mother screamed and came running up behind his father, who was carrying a stick. But before they got to Teddy, Rikki had jumped onto the snake's back, biting as close to the head as he - could. The bite paralyzed the little snake, and Rikki was just about to eat him when he remembered that a full mongoose is a slow mongoose, and he needed to stay thin and quick if he was going to fight Nag and Nagaina.

"You've saved Teddy!" cried Teddy's

mother, gathering Rikki up in her arms and carrying him into the house. Rikki felt proud, of course. But he didn't understand all the fuss. Teddy's mother may as well have petted him for rolling in the dust. He was, after all, enjoying himself.

That night Teddy carried Rikki off to bed with him. But as soon as the boy was asleep, Rikki went on his nightly rounds throughout the house, making sure that all was safe. Round by the wall, he ran into Chuchundra, the muskrat.

"Don't kill me!" cried Chuchundra, for he was a whimpering, fearful creature.

"I do not kill muskrats," Rikki said. "I kill snakes."

"How do I know that Nag won't mistake me for you on one of these dark nights?" Chuchundra said, quivering with fear. "My cousin Chua, the rat, told me —"

"Told you what?" Rikki asked, full of curiosity.

"Shhhh! Nag is everywhere!" Chuchundra replied. "You should have talked to Chua in the garden."

"Tell me, Chuchundra, or I will have to bite you!" Rikki said.

Chuchundra did not answer but sat down and cried. "Can't you *hear*, Rikki-tikki?" he said mournfully.

Rikki-tikki listened. And though the house was still, he could hear the faintest of scratch-scratches — the dry scratch of a snake's scales on bricks.

"That is Nag or Nagaina," Rikki told himself, "crawling into the bathroom pipes." Wasting no time, Rikki scurried off to Teddy's bathroom. There was nothing there. But in Teddy's mother's bathroom, Rikki saw a loose brick and heard hissing voices just outside in the moonlight.

"When the people are gone from this house, the mongoose will leave as well, and the garden will be ours again," Nagaina hissed. "And as soon as our eggs in the melon bed hatch, our children will need space and quiet. The big man is the first to be bitten. When you have done that, come out and tell me, and we shall hunt for Rikki-tikki together."

"I will kill the big man and his wife, and the child if I can," Nag replied.

Rikki's eyes glowed red in the darkness, and he was filled with anger as Nag's head came in through the pipe. But as he watched the five long feet of Nag's cobra body appear, Rikki felt a moment of fear. Nag raised his head, and Rikki could see the snake's glittering eyes.

Nag took a long drink from the big water jar that was used to fill the bath. "I will catch the big man off guard when he comes in to bathe in the morning," he said in a low hiss. "Nagaina, do you hear me? I shall wait here until daytime."

Nagaina did not reply, so Rikki-tikki knew that she had gone away. He watched as Nag slowly coiled and coiled his long body around the bottom of the water jar. Not moving a muscle, Rikki waited.

An hour later Rikki moved, slowly and silently, toward the water jar. In the dark stillness he studied the sleeping cobra and decided he must bite Nag on the head, just above his great hood. If he missed his mark or let go before his bite went deep enough, it would mean bad things for Rikki.

Rikki jumped and landed on Nag's head, sinking his teeth into the snake's flesh as far as he could. At once Nag was awake and furious, lashing his body around the bathroom with tremendous force. Rikki was banged against the floor, the bathtub, and the walls, until he was sure he would be banged to death. But his eyes flamed red, and he did not let go.

Boom! Boom! The noise echoed like thunder in Rikki's ears. A hot wind blew over him and fire singed his fur. The big man had fired two shots at the cobra, just behind the hood.

Rikki closed his eyes, sure he was dead. But it was Nag who did not move. And then the big man picked Rikki up. "It's the mongoose again, Alice," he said. "The little chap has saved *our* lives now." The man petted Rikki and carried him to Teddy's bedroom, where Rikki spent the rest of the night licking his battered body, checking to see if it was as broken as it felt (it wasn't).

In the morning Rikki was stiff and sore but quite pleased with himself. But he knew that his work was not finished.

"I still have Nagaina to take care of, and she will be worse than five Nags," he said to himself. "And then, of course, there are the eggs she spoke of, which will hatch into cobras, too. I must go and see Darzee."

Not waiting for breakfast, Rikki went into the garden to the thornbush where

Darzee had made his nest. The tailorbird was singing a victory song at the top of his lungs, celebrating the news of Nag's death.

"You foolish tuft of feathers," Rikki said, a little bit annoyed. Didn't Darzee realize this was serious business? "You're safe enough up there in your nest, but it's war for me down here. Stop singing a minute."

"I will stop for the great and beautiful Rikki," the bird replied. "What is it, O killer of the terrible Nag, great Rikki-tikki with the white teeth?"

"Where is Nagaina?" Rikki asked, trying not to sound impatient.

"On the garbage heap by the stables, mourning for Nag," Darzee replied.

"And do you know where she keeps her eggs?" Rikki said.

"In the melon bed, on the end nearest the wall, where it is sunny all day." Darzee looked at Rikki sadly. "But, Rikki, you are not going to eat her eggs, are you?" For

Darzee was a foolish bird who did not realize that cobra eggs hatch and grow up to
be dangerous cobras. But his wife, a sensi-
ble bird, knew this to be true. She flew off
to the garbage heap to distract Nagaina so
that Rikki could dispose of the cobra eggs.

"Oh, my wing is broken!" cried Darzee's
wife, fluttering over Nagaina's head.

Nagaina slithered along the dusty
ground toward Darzee's wife. "You
warned Rikki-tikki yesterday when I was
about to kill him," she hissed. "And now
you've chosen a bad place to be lame."

"The boy in the house threw a stone
and broke my wing!" Darzee's wife cried,
sounding desperate.

"Though you will soon be dead, it may
be a consolation to you that tonight the
boy will lie still forever. Little fool, look at
me!"

Darzee's wife knew better than to do
that, for a bird who looks into a snake's
eyes gets so frightened it cannot move. So

instead she fluttered on just above the ground, moaning about her pretend broken wing.

Meanwhile, Rikki hurried to the melon patch, where he found twenty-five whitish cobra eggs, nearly ready to hatch.

Working quickly, Rikki bit off the top of each egg, taking care to crush the cobra inside.

"I am not a day too soon," he told himself. The snakes were about to hatch and, as soon as they did, they would be able to kill both a mongoose and a man.

Rikki had crushed all but three of the unhatched cobra eggs when he heard Darzee's wife scream.

"Rikki!" she shouted. "I led Nagaina - toward the house and she has gone onto the veranda. Come quickly! She means killing!"

Rikki smashed two of the remaining three eggs and picked up the third one in his mouth. Then he raced toward the veranda, where Teddy and his parents were having breakfast. But instead of eating they sat stock-still, their faces white as sheets. Nagaina was coiled at the base of Teddy's chair, swaying her head to and fro and crooning a song of triumph.

"Keep very still, you three," she hissed. "I am not ready yet. If you move I strike, and if you do not move I strike. You foolish people who killed my Nag!"

Teddy stared hard at his father but did not move.

"Nagaina!" Rikki called behind them. "Look! Go look at your eggs in the melon bed!"

The big snake turned halfway around and saw the egg in front of Rikki on the veranda. "Ah-h!" she cried. "Give it to me!"

Rikki's eyes glowed red as he put his paws on either side of the egg. "What price for an egg? For a young cobra? For the last one — the very last of the brood?

The ants are already eating your other children down in the melon bed."

Nagaina spun around, forgetting all about Teddy and his parents. Quick as a flash, Teddy's father grabbed Teddy by the shoulder and pulled him to safety.

"It was I who killed Nag," Rikki said proudly, "for I bit him on the head. And though he tried to throw me off, I held tight. Come then, Nagaina. Come and fight with me."

Nagaina knew that she had lost her opportunity to kill Teddy, and also saw her egg between Rikki's paws.

"Give me the egg, Rikki-tikki," Nagaina said. "Give me the last of my eggs, and I will leave and never come back."

"That is right," Rikki replied. "You will go away and never come back because you are going to the garbage heap with Nag!"

Furious, Nagaina gathered herself together and struck, missing Rikki by inches.

Rikki bounded all around her, his eyes like little red coals. She came at him again and again, missing each time. But Rikki was moving farther and farther away from the egg, while Nagaina was getting closer.

Finally, Nagaina lunged and caught the egg in her mouth. Then, flying like an arrow, she tore down the path toward he hole.

Rikki was fast on her heels. He knew that he had to catch her, or the trouble would begin all over again. But a cobra fleeing for her life is very fast indeed.

As Nagaina and Rikki approached the thornbush, Rikki could hear Darzee still singing his song of triumph. But his wife was smarter and swooped down to distract the escaping cobra. Lowering her hood, Nagaina paused for less than a second and raced on. But that half a second was all Rikki needed to inch closer and, as the cobra slithered into her hole, Rikki locked his teeth around her tail and followed her in, sticking his feet out to slow her progress. But it was deathly dark in the hole, and Rikki did not know when the narrow passageway would open into a chamber and give Nagaina room to turn and strike.

Outside, the grass above the cobra hole stopped waving, and Darzee and his wife looked sorrowfully at the spot where Rikki had disappeared. For though a mongoose occasionally followed a cobra into its hole, it almost never came out again.

"It is all over for Rikki-tikki!" Darzee sang mournfully. "Valiant Rikki-tikki is dead, for Nagaina will certainly kill him underground!"

He sang and sang, making up the words as he went along. And just as he got to the most sentimental part of the song, the grass above the cobra hole quivered again and a very dirty Rikki-tikki-tavi emerged, licking his whiskers.

"It's all over," Rikki said, tired but full of pride. "Nagaina will never come out again." And without another word, he curled up in the grass and went to sleep, for though it was still morning, he had already done a hard day's work.

Much later, when Rikki woke, he asked Darzee to spread the news that Nagaina was dead. Soon birds were singing and frogs were croaking for joy all over the garden.

That night Rikki dined with his human family, eating until he could eat no more. Then he went to bed on Teddy's shoulder, curling up into a ball of fur and sleeping the whole night through. And from that day on, there was never again a cobra in the garden of the big bungalow in Segowlee, India.